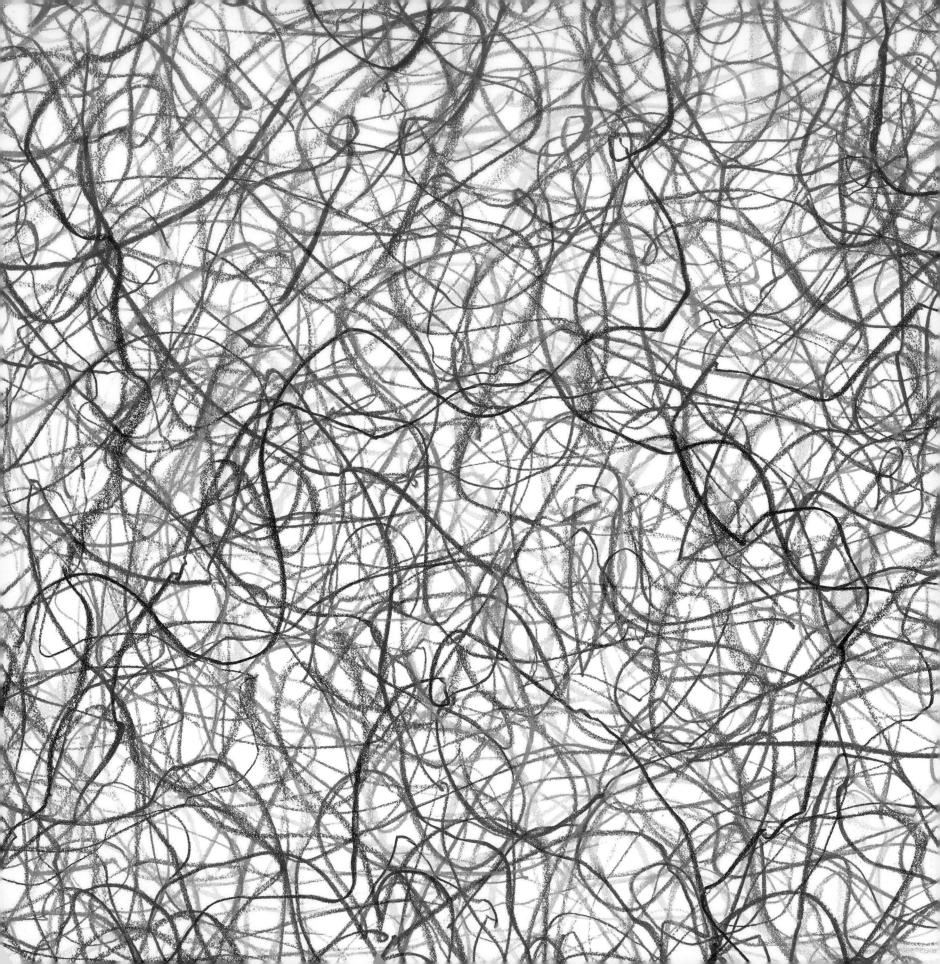

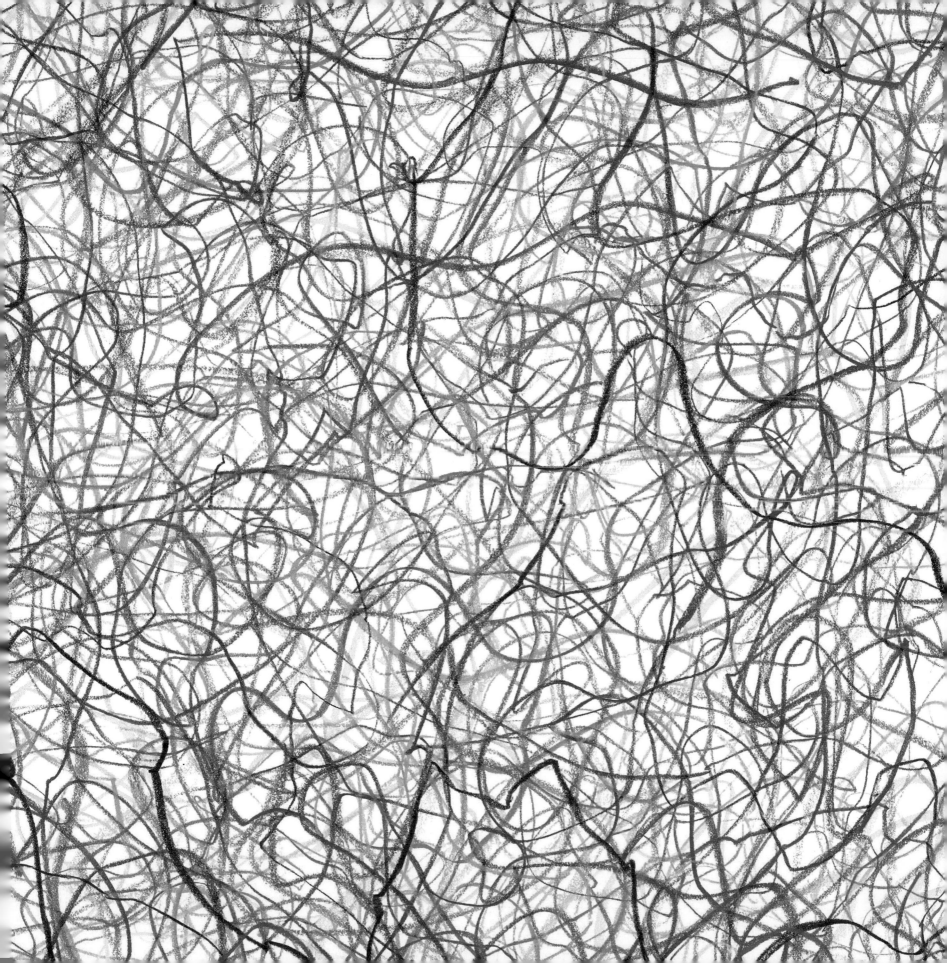

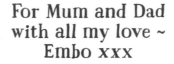

For Mum and Dad
with all my love ~
Embo xxx

Bloomsbury Publishing, London, Oxford, New York, New Delhi and Sydney

First published in Great Britain in 2016 by Bloomsbury Publishing Plc
50 Bedford Square, London, WC1B 3DP

Text and illustrations copyright © Emily MacKenzie 2016
The moral right of the author/illustrator has been asserted

A CIP catalogue record for this book is available from the British Library

ISBN 978 1 4088 6047 2 (HB)
ISBN 978 1 4088 6048 9 (PB)

Printed in China by Leo Paper Products, Heshan, Guangdong

1 3 5 7 9 10 8 6 4 2

www.bloomsbury.com

All papers used by Bloomsbury Publishing are natural, recyclable products
made from wood grown in well-managed forests.
The manufacturing processes conform to the environmental regulations of the country of origin

Stanley

the
Amazing Knitting Cat

Emily MacKenzie

BLOOMSBURY

LONDON OXFORD NEW YORK NEW DELHI SYDNEY

Stanley wasn't like other cats. He didn't enjoy
chasing mice. He was very friendly to passing dogs.
And he never lazed around, dozing in the sunshine.

No, Stanley liked to be crafty,
but not in a sneaky way...

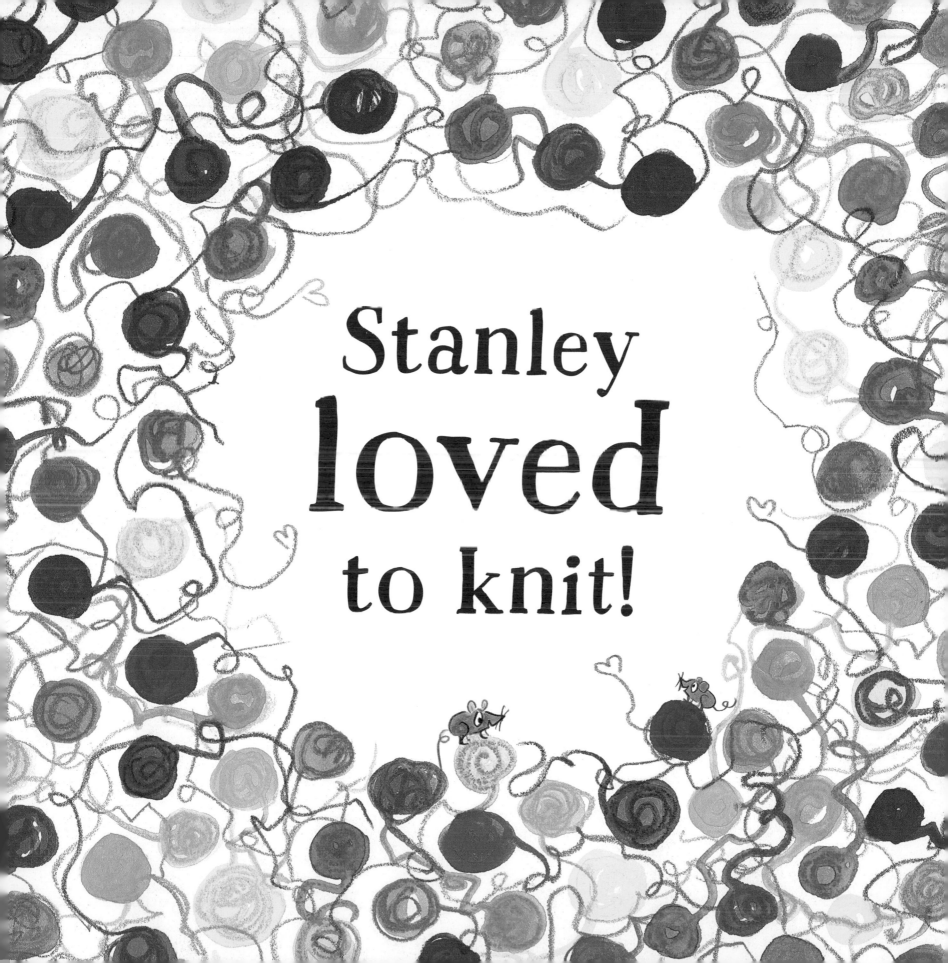

Stanley
loved
to knit!

He knocked up **pompoms** at breakfast time,

whipped up **bobble hats** at bathtime.

He knitted **tail cosies** at the supermarket.

Stanley **even** knitted **on the bus!**

And what did Stanley do with all his woolly creations?
He gave them to his friends, of course!

He made **balaclavas** for the bunnies...

...neck warmers
for the giraffes,

trunk tubes
for the elephants

and plenty of
jolly jumpers,

silly socks

and
woolly onesies.

Yes, Stanley could knit anything and everything.
So when he spotted a poster one day,
he knew what he had to do.

Stanley got knitting straight away.
But **what** was he making?

CLICKETY-KNIT! TWIRLY-TWIST!

"It's a
woolly jelly!"
said Giraffe.

"It's a
giant carrot!"
said Rabbit.

"Definitely the **longest woolly
rainbow** in the **world!**" said Monkey.

POM-POM-PULL! CLACKETY-CLICK! BOBBLY-BITS! TWIDDLY-LOOPY-WOOL! CLICKETY-KNIT! TWIRLY-TWIST! POM-POM-PULL!

But Stanley said nothing.
He just kept **knitting** and **knitting** until . . .

...one day the clicking suddenly stopped.
Stanley had completely **run out** of wool —
and the competition was the very next day!
What could he do? How was he going to find more wool in time?

Stanley looked at his friends.
He couldn't — could he?
Surely not!

But he could! Oh, yes he could!

The great **unravelling** began.

Stanley was **delighted**. He had enough wool all right!

brrrr!

BRRR!

BEARS
THIS
WAY →

But Stanley's friends **weren't** quite so happy.

BRRR!

The next day, Stanley's chilly friends gathered with the crowds
at the Town Hall, eager to view the woolly wonders.
There were...

woolly dragons,

dinosaurs,

cuddly
toadstools

and **giant** knitted cakes.

But no sign of Stanley **or** his woolly wonder.

"He'll never win now," shivered Giraffe.
"It's all been a waste of time," added Rabbit, his teeth chattering.

But then...

CRASH!
BANG!
THUD!

Everyone rushed outside — and there was Stanley **IN** his wonderfully woolly creation!
"What are you waiting for? **All aboard!**" he cried.

"But what about the competition?" asked Giraffe.

"That can wait," said Stanley.
"You, my friends, are far more important.
I'm **sorry** I took **your woollies.**"

Up, up and away!

Everyone climbed aboard and off they went.

And Stanley and his friends didn't have to wait long before they heard the most exciting news.

"The **winner** of the **Woolly Wonders Competition** is...

Stanley the Amazing Knitting Cat!

A lifetime's supply of wool goes to you."

Which was just as well.
Because now his friends were even more
woolly and even more **wonderful**
than ever before!

BOBBLY-BITS! TWIDDLY-LOOPY-WOOL! CLICKETY-KNIT TW

CLICKETY-KNIT! TWIRLY-TWIST! POM-POM-PULL! CLICKETY-CLICK!

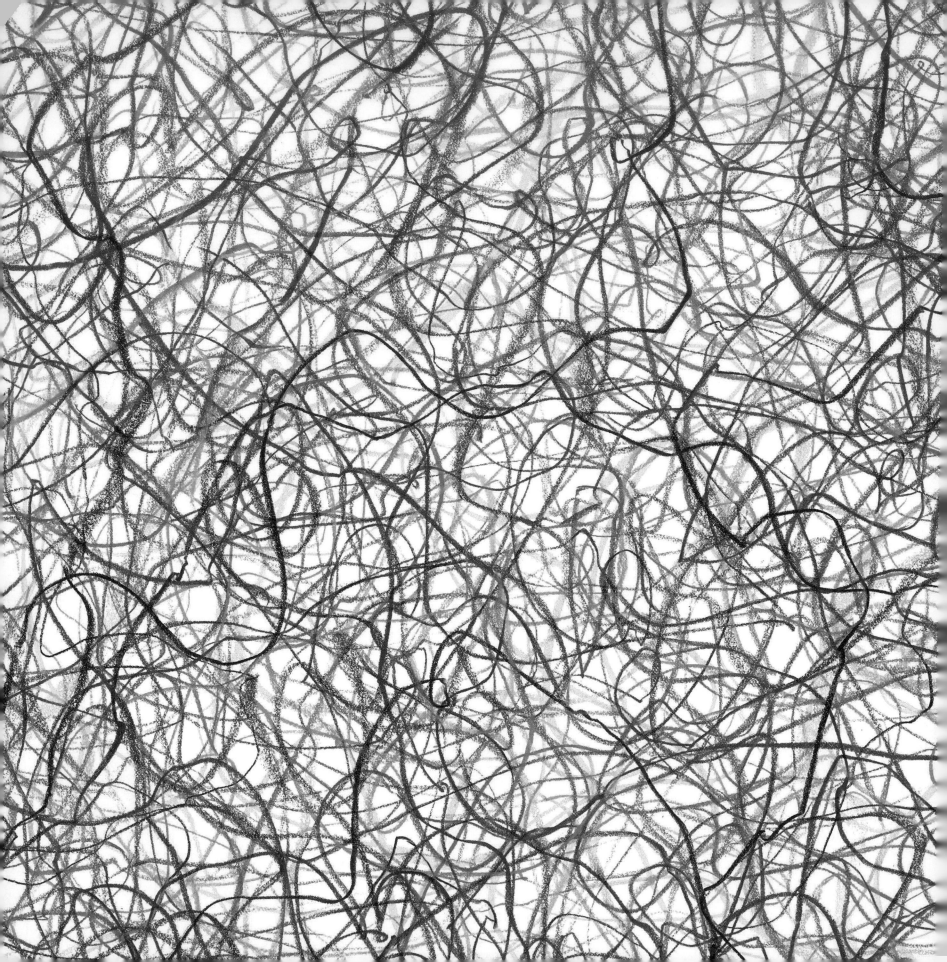

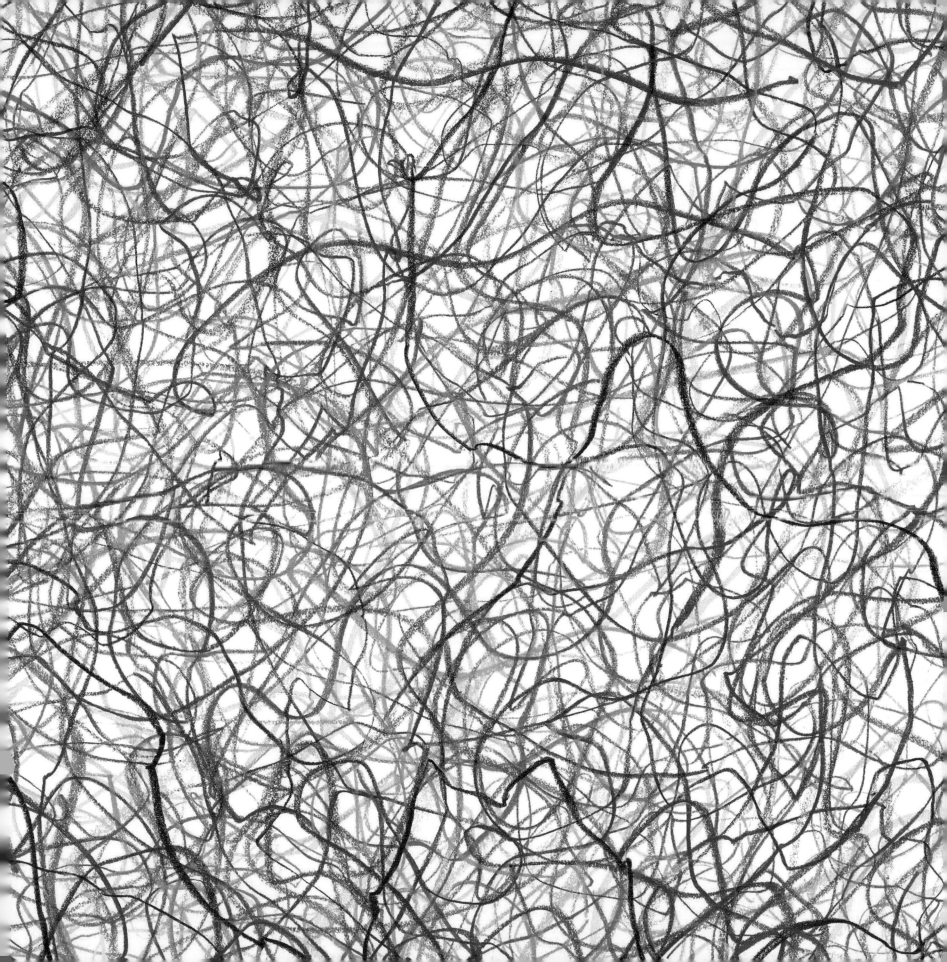

The End